NURSING REFLECTIONS

CAROLYN CHRISTINE DEW

Order this book online at www.trafford.com
or email orders@trafford.com

Most Trafford titles are also available at major online book retailers.

Print information available on the last page.

ISBN: 978-1-6987-0944-4 (sc)
ISBN: 978-1-6987-0945-1 (e)

Library of Congress Control Number: 2021918523

Trafford rev. 01/25/2022

 www.trafford.com

North America & international
toll-free: 844-688-6899 (USA & Canada)
fax: 812 355 4082

CONTENTS

DEDICATION

For the nurses who work so hard and give so much to patients and the profession. This work would not be possible if it were not for the patients, colleagues, and families who are a great part of this work. I want to dedicate this book to my daughter, Christina Ramos; my son and his partner, Sam Taylor and Naomi Greenberg; my granddaughter, Taylor Ramos, who is in Pre Nursing, and to my grandson, Luke Ramos. This work is a labor of love and a wonderful way to remember an exciting and blessed career in nursing.

It's Just Henry

There is never a dull moment in the life of a home health nurse. She visited an old, black lady who lives alone in the woods to provide medication teaching for hypertension. The nurse assessed her patient and her Vital Signs and completed her teaching plan.

The lady requested to change her clothes and asked the nurse to reach inside the chest of drawers for some clothing. The little house was dimly lit. The nurse reached into a drawer for the clothing and to her surprise, suddenly she felt something move that was cold and leathery. The nurse cried out in fear. The patient responded with, "It's just Henry! He is my black snake who just hangs around in my drawers. He won't hurt you."

The nurse was mortified with fear and shaken to her core. Who would have expected Henry, the black snake to be comfortably nestled in some clothes in a drawer?

Her patient had learned to co-exist with a creature who was quite comfortable in a very unlikely place.

BLIND SPOT-ON

The nurse visited a gentleman who was blind for the purpose of assessing her patient, checking his blood sugar, and teaching diabetic care. She made herself comfortable in a wooden chair in the little dirty, wooden shack.

The patient dipped snuff as his habit and all of a sudden, he let go of a large spit bomb of snuff spittle that landed in a hole in the wooden floor, just where the nurse was sitting. He was blind but he was able to hit the target of the hole with exceptional ease.

The nurse mused to herself that even with two good eyes wide open to see, she could not hit that hole in the floor like her blind patient did with very little effort on his part. What a surprise feat of the blind spot-on!

KILLING ME SOFTLY

The hospice nurse had a wonderful opportunity to be a patient advocate. As she worked with her patient who was Gay and dying with AIDS, she learned, that he wanted very much to have his favorite song played at his funeral. His partner, who had already passed, shared his love for that song. It was their song. He also knew in his heart of hearts that his family and friends might not appreciate his last wishes. The nurse assured him she would assist in working out his wish with the family.

The patient died and the nurse helped to fulfill the patient's last request by discussing it with the family and the pastor. The pastor and the family were unsettled about it but the nurse boldly advocated for her patient. They decided they would have the song played during the viewing and receiving of friends and family. The patient's request was honored and "Killing Me Softly With His Song" was played as planned. Perceptions and views may be very different from your own but, a family member's last wishes can be granted with much grace and love because it was the right thing to do.

HIV in The 80'S

A nurse is presented with many challenges in his or her career when science has not caught up with the times. Diseases come on the scene and the community is not always prepared for the best care. This was the case in the 1980's with HIV AIDS impacting a rural community in a southern state.

A black gentleman who was Gay contracted HIV when he lived up North. He came home to die in a small, southern community. His family had abandoned him and he lived alone in a small single-wide mobile home.

Like many southern, rural communities, services were not available or adequately provided for a challenging patient with a serious disease like AIDS. Many home health agencies would not accept the challenging patients and the community was not yet prepared to manage the care.

One very brave and courageous home health supervisor intentionally decided to accept a referral from a tertiary medical center. She made the decision to care for the patient herself since she wanted to be the role model for her staff. She believed in letting her staff see that she was willing to care for the patient first before she expected them to do it.

The patient experienced such loneliness, grief and depression. He knew he was near the end and on one occasion attempted to end his life himself. He started a fire in the middle of the floor of the mobile home with some wood and other articles. The heap melted and he lost his nerve to complete the act.

The nurse arrived to assess the patient and she saw the melted area in the middle of the floor. Sometimes, words are not needed and the quiet presence of a caring nurse can speak volumes. They talked about his fears, the grief, the lonely hours, and any conversation the patient needed to have.

The patient began hemorrhaging from his rectal area. The nurse donned her protective equipment and prepared her patient. She contacted the physician and called for the emergency service. The physician would have him come to the hospital if the patient chose to come. The emergency service said they had other calls and by the time they would have arrived, the patient would have exsanguinated. The nurse remained at the bedside and made him as comfortable as possible. She held his hand and wiped his forehead and never left him alone. He died with the nurse who did not abandon him. They talked and cried–living and dying.

She had another fight on her hands with the funeral home director because there was so much blood. They finally picked up his body and would cremate the patient. Resistance was real because the science of the disease had not caught up with policies, procedures, and protocols. Medical personnel and allied services were fearful.

There is a healing that can take place with the brave and courageous heart of a willing nurse. A death like this is a hard experience but a nurse who is willing to be a pioneer in the care of a complicated case, can move things forward. Times have changed and so much progress has been made in the care of AIDS. Patients are living longer, knowledge has increased, treatments work, and society's acceptance is progressing.

Angel of Death

The on-call hospice nurse can be a tough experience at times. The nights can be long and grueling and the nurse has to endure difficult situations. It happened one night that the nurse received a call to visit a dying patient and she responded with all her skills and her nursing bag.

She provided hospice comfort measures for her patient and the family. When the last breath occurred from her patient, she made the call to the physician and reported the death. She remained with the family until the funeral director received the body.

Another call came in and the hospice nurse visited the patient. She assessed her patient and realized the patient had expired. She comforted the family and called the physician to report the patient's demise. She prepared the body and waited with the family until the funeral director came to receive the body.

Oh what a night! Another call came in for the nurse to come to the patient's home to provide hospice care. The patient took her last breath within

30 minutes of the arrival of the hospice nurse. She pronounced the patient's death and called the physician to report it. It happened to be the same physician as in the other two previous deaths. He exclaimed jokingly to the hospice nurse, "What are you doing to all of my patients? Who are you, the angel of death?"

This was a fateful night for this very caring hospice nurse. The physician helped to bring a little balance to the difficult situation for the nurse. Losing one patient is hard but losing three in one night can be hard to bear. The nurse thanked the physician for the humor and told him she hoped she would not have to call him again.

THE FLY CATCHER

A public health nurse was assigned to visit a young, disabled and mentally challenged boy. He lived in a rural, farming community with his parents who were also mentally challenged but were able to function at home.

The nurse arrived and entered the home. She noted unpleasant odors of old, dirty clothes. As she was moving across the room, she saw a huge, brown, wharf rat as big as a cat, moving back and forth behind an old smelly couch. This startled and frightened the nurse and she became very talkative. She feared the rat would do more than move back and forth. About the same time, a fly was darting about her face, and all of a sudden, she sucked the fly in and could feel the whirring wings of the fly in her throat. The mother began pounding on the back of the nurse. She said, "I am so sorry you swallowed one of our flies. I hope you don't get sick." The nurse told the mother, "Please leave the fly where he is. Believe me, we do not want him to come up again."

All the nurse could think about was, where had that fly landed before she sucked him in. The nurse had always reminisced that this was her badge of courage for being a public health nurse. She would never forget this incident in her nursing career.

Spirit in This House

The nurse aide and the home health nurse agreed to make a joint home visit to the home of a frail, elderly, black lady. They planned to bathe the patient to help one another. The nurse could observe and assess the patient's skin.

When they arrived at the home, all of the family members were congregated on the front porch. A family member ran to the nurse's car and made a distressing request for the nurse to come quickly to check Grandma. The family members seemed to be quite anxious and upset.

When the nurse assessed the patient, she observed that the patient was cold, very stiff with rigor mortis, and ashen in color. Apparently, the patient had expired in the early morning hours and the family discovered her condition and they moved to the front porch until the nurse and aide arrived.

The caring nurses provided the post-mortem care and called the doctor to report the death. They stayed with the family until the funeral director came to receive the body. The family wanted the nurse to call the equipment company immediately to pick up the hospital bed. They said they were worried about the spirit coming into the house with the bed still there. The nurse honored the family's request and called the equipment company to pick up the bed as soon as possible.

When death occurred in this home, the family's culture caused them to be unsettled and upset. Some of the family members left the home completely and the others stayed on the porch. The nurse tried to reassure the family, but they were coping with it in their own way until the hospital bed could be removed.

Uninvited Guests

An elderly, black gentleman had a Venous Stasis Ulcer on his right lower leg and the nurse visited two times a week to dress his wound. She would remove the old dressing, cleanse the leg, and apply a compression bandage wrap to decrease the swelling in his leg.

One hot summer afternoon, the nurse and patient decided to do the dressing change on the patient's back porch. The nurse assessed the vital signs and proceeded to change the dressing. She made plans to return later in the week and dress the wound again.

On the next visit, the patient was quite distressed relaying the fact that the right leg was stinging, itching, and very uncomfortable. When the nurse removed the bandage, both nurse and patient were amazed and very surprised to find that there were maggots working in the wound. The nurse went about her work and cleansed the wound and they found that the uninvited guests had done a remarkable job with cleaning the wound of debris. They had debrided the wound much better than a surgeon would have done. The uninvited guests had really made an invaluable and healing contribution to the patient's care.

TERROR IN THE PSYCH WARD

The evening supervisor was making her rounds on the psychiatric ward. She unlocked the door on the outside with her keys and then locked the door on the inside. The ward was eerily quiet and there was no one in sight. As she was processing the scene, she asked the question, "Where is everybody?"

At the end of a long hall, she saw a large woman coming to meet her like the speed of a freight train. The woman and the nurse were eye-to-eye, facing each other. The nurse asked the woman, "Where is everybody?" The large woman told the nurse, "I scared all of those cowards. I scared the hell out of them and they ran away. Now, I am going to knock the hell out of you too."

The nurse stared into the woman's eyes with absolute confidence, and said, "You do not want to do that!" The patient drew back a fist and aimed it and just barely touched the nurse's forehead. She cried out with a belly-laugh and the nurse joined her and said, "Let's go find those cowards and get you something

23

to drink." They went down the hall arm-in-arm in search of the staff and other patients.

The supervisor saw all the overturned tables and chairs that looked like a war zone. The staff reported that the patient was agitated and started yelling obscenities and turning over tables and chairs and everyone had taken cover. The patients had hidden under beds and in closets. The staff took cover in the locked nurse's station from the terror that had gripped them. Everyone came out of their safe places and the terror on the psych ward had finally resolved and safety was restored.

ALEXA GIVES THE ANSWER

During the COVID pandemic, nursing classes were conducted online. The nursing professor held her clinical class on Zoom with ten students. They were exploring the topic of potassium deficiency related to a patient scenario.

The professor asked one of the students who happened to be named Alexa, to describe the signs and symptoms of potassium deficiency to the class. While the student had paused to collect her thoughts, Alexa from the Echo-Dot device in the professor's office, answered the question. She said, "According to Wikipedia, the signs and symptoms of potassium deficiency are weakness, fatigue, muscle cramps, and abnormal heart rhythms."

The whole class erupted in laughter and enjoyed the very humorous moment in their class. Who would have thought that Alexa from Echo-Dot would have joined in the class discussion and contributed such valuable information?

THE LAST UTTERANCE

It is a common expectation among night nurses who work in the nursing home that patient deaths occur in the night. This was the case on one dark night, when the night nurse and two nursing assistants experienced the death of a patient.

They had completed their post-mortem care and took the patient by stretcher to the chapel to await the funeral director who would receive the body. As they were about to leave the chapel and had turned off the light, the patient let out a very loud gasp of air, "Uggggg!" The nursing assistants ran out of the chapel and all one could see was a blur of the color of their uniforms flying down the dimly lit hall to escape in fear. One could say that the patient had the last word in this case as the last utterance.

Go for It!

A young, energetic, and idealistic home health supervisor had an awesome idea to start a hospice since there was a great need for the service in this large, rural county. The nearest hospice was 30 miles away. She proposed the idea to her district nursing director who said to the young nurse, "Go for it!"

She made a plan to consider all the parts that would have to be addressed. What a project this would be. She had to sell the idea to grassroots organizations and political players in the community. Policies and procedures would have to be made. The hospice team and volunteers would have to be recruited and trained. The whole community was involved in the project and they worked diligently on all the pieces for 3 years.

Under her caring leadership, the hospice found a home within the public health department home health agency. The first patients were served and the state performed the initial survey for Medicare and Medicaid certification to be used for reimbursement sources. The home health and hospice agency is still fully functioning and licensed to serve the residents of that rural county today.

The words of the district nursing director were empowering and dynamic and they matched the idealism and heart of that young supervisor. "Go for it!"

BEFORE GPS

How did a home health and hospice nurse handle directions to the homes of patients before GPS? The common way in those days in town was to use the numbers on the houses and mailboxes or describe something unique about the house. The rural areas could be challenging. The patients would give directions such as turn right at the old red barn or the dirt path with the green mailbox. Sometimes, the direction given was to make a turn at the two stumps or the tractor in the yard, at the big oak tree, and the yellow house with the blue door.

The nurse would use her skills of creativity and observation for details. She would make it a fun activity to find the patient and use her vivid imagination. GPS is a real asset now, but it will never surpass a nurse's creativity and ingenuity. When the nurse reflects upon those heartwarming times, she realizes how much she has learned about her patient's community and the beauty of the landscapes on her travels. The challenge was well worth the effort.

ROLE REVERSAL

The young high school student worked for two summers at the local hospital to earn some income for her education and to see if nursing would be a fit for her. She worked with two very good nursing aides. They formed a bond and she learned many things from them.

The student graduated from high school and went to nursing school. She graduated and passed the state board to get her nursing license. Her first job was evening duty at the same hospital she worked in as a nurse aide. She was given the nursing position on evening duty and the two nurse aides she had worked side-by-side with would work with her again. What a dilemma this would be. The young nurse would have to establish herself as the nurse in charge on the evening shift.

She intentionally worked side-by-side with the two nurse aides and vowed to never have the attitude that she would not empty a bedpan or get her hands dirty. She respected her two assistants and involved them in the work on the unit to praise them for their skills. She treated them like she wanted to be treated.

The strategy worked and they functioned well as a team. The new charge nurse established herself as a leader in their eyes. What a win-win for all of them!

A Graceful Exit

The nurse made a home visit in a known, high crime area of the city on the weekend. Her assignment was to teach a new diabetic patient. She entered the home and set up her care space to assess and teach her new patient. She was well into her teaching plan when an obviously inebriated gentleman came into the room and stood directly in front of the nurse and her patient. He folded his arms across his chest and propped himself against the wall.

She continued to teach and another man who was also intoxicated entered the room and stood next to the first man. By now, the nurse had become a little uncomfortable but she wanted to complete her task.

Another man came from the next room and he stood against the wall too. It was not long before the fourth intoxicated man came and they began getting loud and asking the nurse to check their blood pressures. The nurse promptly told her patient that the teaching plan was done for the day. She spoke to the four intoxicated men and told them she would be glad to take their blood pressures the next time she came if they were there. She gracefully gathered her nursing bag and teaching materials and backed out of the room with a big smile.

"Big Mac"

Nurses have the challenge, sometimes, to care for bariatric patients. She had a patient who weighed 565 pounds in her caseload. He spent his days in bed on two mattresses which were on a very large platform. He always looked so miserable and uncomfortable. Since he never left his surroundings, the family brought food into the home for him. This seemed to be the only thing he enjoyed was his food and he manipulated, coerced, and made his family feel guilty for not bringing him what he wanted.

The nurse tried to work with the family to make dietary changes so the patient could lose weight but he refused to cooperate. They would bring him fast food in huge quantities and it was going to lead to a poor outcome for the patient.

On one visit, the nurse observed the patient eat four Big Macs, three large french fries, and a huge soft drink with refills. As one would expect, the patient had earned his name as "Big Mac". The physician had to visit the patient in his own surroundings because the patient could not go outside his home. The emergency medical service was not really equipped with bariatric equipment, therefore it was an impossible task to lift him without special equipment.

One day, Big Mac became very ill and died in his home. It was truly a challenge to care for a bariatric patient in the early 2000s. We have come far now with special lifting devices, wheelchairs, beds, and other equipment. We have better knowledge of how to care for patients like "Big Mac" with better outcomes.

A THREE-DOG DAY

T he home health nurse cannot always predict what she may face during a nursing visit to a home. An example of this is a nurse who had to make a visit to a patient in his home and just outside the door, there were three large, angry Pit Bulls chained nearby. When the nurse knocks, the dogs go crazy with loud barking and pulling against the chains. The nurse thinks to herself, if those chains break, I am going to be hurt for sure.

No one answered the door so the nurse left and called her manager. The manager called the patient and let him know it was not safe for the nurse to visit unless the dogs could be secured. It would be his responsibility to secure the dogs if he wanted the service. The plan would be for the nurse to call and then the patient would secure the dogs and the nurse could provide the services ordered by the physician. The patient agreed to the plan.

A Safe
House Story

Working in a Christian Domestic Violence Shelter poses different challenges and experiences. A pregnant mother, her three-year-old daughter, and five-year-old son came to the shelter and it was a difficult situation for them and the advocate worker. The father who was the abuser was the father of the unborn child, the daughter but not the son's father. The son was very jealous of the sister and he exhibited very violent tendencies. He would push and strike his sister and hurt her. He disobeyed his mother by climbing onto the table and defying her by not getting down as she asked him to do. His behavior was very unpredictable and stormy. He would yell loudly and refuse to stop. The mother and daughter were very anxious and ignored his bad behavior.

The advocate had to intervene when he hit his mother in the stomach very hard and she doubled over with pain. The advocate steered him into a corner and told him he was out of control and the behavior would no longer be tolerated. He tried to loosen himself and bite the advocate. The advocate called the manager of the shelter and the manager arranged for the family to be transferred to another facility. The mother was upset and cried over and over that if they were home, he would not behave this way. The advocate asked why this would be so, and the mother admitted that the father would beat him and the son would obey. For the safety of all in the Safe House, the family was transferred to a more appropriate facility. The mother released her daughter to the husband and she and the son moved to another state.

It is Okay to Be Different

A Safe House admits families with diverse backgrounds, races, ethnicities, and religions. One experience in the Safe House reveals how it was able to cope with the differences. A mother and her two young sons were Hasidic Jews and another mother and her son were Muslim. The advocate who worked with them identified as Christian.

The three religions came together and shared their beliefs, customs, clothing, food, and traditions. Each one respected the differences and they were able to find common ground with each other.

The Safe House established a safe place to share very different views. The spirit in the group was welcoming and loving. Each person learned about the others' beliefs, traditions, food, clothing and customs. There was no fear or being uncomfortable with each other. It was a sweet, precious fellowship with others who were different from you but yet, you could become a part of them in your pain as the common ground.

A Letter for My Nurse

An interesting story happened in a state psychiatric facility. A patient developed a special interest in a nurse who cared for him. He had a phenomenon of transference in which a patient redirects emotions or feelings about one person to an entirely separate individual. He would be near the door when the nurse would enter or exit and he would have a letter for her from him. The handwriting was not even a script. It consisted of wavy lines on the page. It could not be read.

The nurse wanted to be therapeutic therefore, she did not want to encourage the behavior and she did not want him to be rejected. She made a plan to sit with him in the dayroom where she could be under supervision to explore what the patient needed to say to her. She desired to build trust, show empathy, but act professionally. She made a request to him to not write her a letter but if he needed to talk with her, she would meet with him to discuss his concerns. The behavior stopped and the patient was improving in his communication.

Teaching Online During Covid-19

Nurses have learned to be adept at teaching online during the COVID-19 pandemic. The nurse who teaches fundamental skills has to be creative. The students are not in a lab where they can learn skills on manikins or demonstrate nursing skills by working with each other. The Nurse Educator utilizes clinical expertise and medical knowledge to equip the next generation.

Nursing is a well-developed discipline that has been forced to adapt to a virtual environment during the pandemic. They have learned new technical skills to use in a remote setting. The curriculum had to be restructured so the student would be able to navigate and have order to the course.

Nursing competencies and skills could be reviewed in class by utilizing a step-by-step format and the students would incorporate the competencies and skills into their nursing practice. In a remote learning environment, students could learn the regulations, policies, and core practices in addition to the technical skills. Instruction could also be provided on cultural competencies and religious practices. Diversity and equality are important in providing quality care.

It takes trial and error to develop a comfortable teaching style online. The teacher has to make a concerted effort to engage all the students by asking questions and directing them individually to make contributions to the discussions. Communication is very important with students. Responding to student questions is imperative and ideally, it should be within 24 hours. If there are problems arising, individual communication to the student shows interest and understanding of their learning needs.

Many strategies can be utilized to facilitate active learning. Pre-class assignments work very well to have the student be prepared before the class and to maximize learning. Case studies can illustrate and demonstrate concepts needing to be learned such as diagnoses, lab studies, medications, and treatments. Providing question banks for students to practice can facilitate learning and provide evaluation of the learning process. Concept Maps map out the nursing care and nursing process. Role playing is useful since the students can be a patient or a caregiver and practice therapeutic communication. Virtual simulation is excellent to provide a case study to practice skills, interpret lab results, administer medications, and provide nursing care. It also provides a time for reflection about the care they provided and how they feel about that care.

Teaching online is a wonderful way to provide nursing education. The learning curve was steep but with the nurse educator's tools, technology, and strategies, the learning process was enhanced and provided with quality.